D1460070

Three Blind Mice

Team Up with the

Three Little Pigs

written by Paul Harrison

illustrated by Mariano Epelbaum

Essex County Council

3013021224718 2

2

Once upon a time, there were three little pigs. They all lived happily in their own homes, until the Big Bad Wolf arrived.

The Big Bad Wolf wanted to eat the pigs. He huffed, and he puffed, and he blew down two of the homes!

The three pigs decided to move into one home together.

The house was very nice, but it had been built for one pig. There just wasn't enough space in the home.

To make matters worse, the Big Bad Wolf was still around. He was still hungry for the pigs.

The pigs wanted to leave their small home, but it was too dangerous to leave. The Big Bad Wolf surely would eat them! What's more, the pigs were running out of food.

8

On the other side of the forest, three blind mice lived in a farmhouse. The house was lovely and warm. The mice had plenty of food.

But the house was too big for mice who couldn't find their way round.

To make matters worse, the house was owned by Mrs Farmer. She did not like the three blind mice.

She would chase the mice up, down and all around to try and chop off their tails.

One day Mrs Farmer chased the mice out of their house. Out in the woods, they bumped into the three pigs. The pigs had **sneaked** out of the house to find food.

The mice and the pigs told each other their sorry stories.

"I think I have a plan," said one of the pigs.

14

As part of the plan, the mice dressed up like the little pigs and went to the pigs' home. That very day, the wolf climbed down the chimney.

He couldn't believe what he saw!

"Pah!" he said. "The pigs have **shrunk** away to nothing. They would not even be a good snack any more!"

And off he stomped.

As part of the plan, the pigs dressed up like the mice and went to their farmhouse.

When Mrs Farmer saw them, she nearly lost her **bloomers** in shock.

"Mice as big as pigs!" she cried.

And off she ran,
never to return.

18

So the three blind mice lived in the pigs' home. It was small and **cosy**. They could easily find their way around.

The three little pigs lived in the farmhouse, which had plenty of room.

And they all lived happily ever after.

The Three Little Pigs

The story of *The Three Little Pigs* told by Joseph Jacobs in 1890 is probably the best known. In Jacobs' story, the three pigs each make a house. One is made of straw, one is made of twigs and one is made of bricks. The wolf blows down the first two houses, but can't blow down the third. He tries to climb down the chimney to catch the pig. He lands in a big cooking pot the pig has put over the fire.

Three Blind Mice

"Three Blind Mice" is a popular children's nursery rhyme from Great Britain. In the rhyme, three blind mice are chased around a house by the farmer's wife. She wants to cut off their tails. The rhyme was first written in 1609, but the one people know today comes from the 1800s.

Glossary

bloomers – big knickers

cosy – warm and comfortable

shrunk – got smaller

sneaked – to creep without being seen

Writing prompts

Try telling the story from the wolf's point of view. What would the wolf say about what happened?

Write some directions for the three blind mice, telling them how to get through the forest to the three little pigs' house. Remember: they can't see where they are going! Think of the other senses: hearing, touch, smell and taste.

Imagine Mrs Farmer told her story to the newspaper. Write the newspaper article.

Read more

Blow Your Nose, Big Bad Wolf (Fairy Tales Gone Wrong)
Steve Smallman (QED, 2015)

The Three Little Pigs (Well-loved Tales), Vera Southgate
(Ladybird, 2015)

The Three Little Wolves and the Big Bad Pig, Euene Trivizas
(Egmont, 2015)

Three Blind Mice (Tangled Tunes), Blake Hoena (Cantata
Learning, 2016)

Websites

www.shortkidstories.com/authors/joseph-jacobs
Read more stories by Joseph Jacobs. He wrote *The Three Little Pigs* story that is well known.

www.smartkids123.com
Read more bedtime stories and fables on this website.

**www.sparklebox.co.uk/literacy/fairytales/three-little-pigs.
html#.Vjcs5q7hCi7**
There are fun activities about *The Three Little Pigs* to print on this website.

Read all the books in the series:

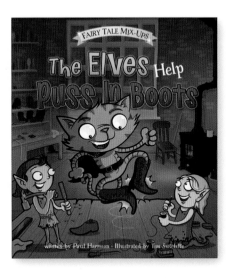

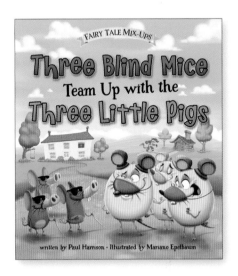

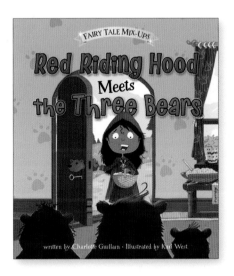

Visit www.raintree.co.uk

Raintree is an imprint of Capstone Global Library Limited, a company incorporated in England and Wales having its registered office at 264 Banbury Road, Oxford, OX2 7DY – Registered company number: 6695582

www.raintree.co.uk
myorders@raintree.co.uk

Text © Capstone Global Library Limited 2017
The moral rights of the proprietor have been asserted.

All rights reserved. No part of this publication may be reproduced in any form or by any means (including photocopying or storing it in any medium by electronic means and whether or not transiently or incidentally to some other use of this publication) without the written permission of the copyright owner, except in accordance with the provisions of the Copyright, Designs and Patents Act 1988 or under the terms of a licence issued by the Copyright Licensing Agency, Saffron House, 6–10 Kirby Street, London EC1N 8TS (www.cla.co.uk). Applications for the copyright owner's written permission should be addressed to the publisher.

Edited by Penny West
Designed by Steve Mead
Original illustrations © Capstone Global Library Ltd 2016
Illustrated by Mariano Epelbaum, Astound US
Production by Steve Walker
Originated by Capstone Global Library Limited
Printed and bound in China

ISBN 978 1 474 72753 2
20 19 18 17 16
10 9 8 7 6 5 4 3 2 1

British Library Cataloguing in Publication Data
A full catalogue record for this book is available from the British Library.

Every effort has been made to contact copyright holders of material reproduced in this book. Any omissions will be rectified in subsequent printings if notice is given to the publisher.

All the Internet addresses (URLs) given in this book were valid at the time of going to press. However, due to the dynamic nature of the Internet, some addresses may have changed, or sites may have changed or ceased to exist since publication. While the author and publisher regret any inconvenience this may cause readers, no responsibility for any such changes can be accepted by either the author or the publisher.